Magnificent
MABEL
and the Very Important Witch

Ruth
Quayle

Julia
Christians

First published in the UK in 2021 by Nosy Crow Ltd
The Crow's Nest, 14 Baden Place,
Crosby Row, London SE1 1YW

www.nosycrow.com

ISBN: 978 1 83994 014 9

Text © Ruth Quayle, 2021
Illustrations © Julia Christians, 2021

A CIP catalogue record for this book is available from the British Library.

Printed and bound in the UK by Clays Ltd, Elcograf S.p.A.

Papers used by Nosy Crow are made from wood grown in sustainable forests.

1 3 5 7 9 10 8 6 4 2

MIX
Paper from
responsible sources
FSC® C018072
www.fsc.org

www.nosycrow.com

1

Magnificent Mabel
and the
Very Important Witch

I'll tell you what is nearly as good as Christmas. Halloween, that's what.

At Halloween you get to carve a pumpkin and you can buy face paint that looks like blood.

At Halloween, you don't even have to say please when you want sweets. You just knock on people's doors and say "Trick or Treat" in a loud voice because on Halloween it's good to be loud. (Except you still have to say thank you when people give you sweets, otherwise you might have to go home early.)

All year long, I count down

the days to Halloween.

Like for instance I love planning what I am going to wear.

I love getting my orange Trick or Treat pot ready.

I love practising my face paint when Mum isn't keeping an eye on her make-up bag.

Last week on Monday I was so happy because it was finally Halloween.

At school everyone in my class was talking about it and SOME people were quite boasty.

Sophie Simpson told me that her dad had bought her a witch outfit in a shop and it cost A LOT of money because it came with a real broomstick that could FLY.

Edward
Silitoe said
he had the
best skeleton
costume ever because
his mum had painted skeleton
bones on a black leotard and
leggings and all the bones were
in the right place
because his mum
is a doctor.

Elsa Kavinsky said she had twenty-four pumpkins outside her house.

But even though everyone was being quite boasty I didn't mind because I remembered that Mum and Dad were taking me and my sister Meg Trick or Treating later and we were going to a street where all the houses are covered in cobwebs. Also, I was dressing up as a werewolf and I couldn't help remembering that werewolves eat skeletons.

I told everybody about my
werewolf costume. I described
the black pointy paws and
the furry brown coat and the
scratchy brown bear head and
I didn't mention
that everything
was from our
dressing-up box
because Sophie
Simpson is used to

things that you buy from shops with real money.

"Wow, Mabel," said Sophie Simpson. "How much did it cost?" And I said, "A lot" and stared out of the window.

I was SO happy.

But when it was home time something stopped me feeling happy and that something was Mum.

After school she had a fidgety smile on her face. She put her arm round me and Meg and then she told us some tragic news.

She said that Dad was held
up at work and she had just had
a phone call from Great-Aunt
Bridget's care home. She said that
Great-Aunt Bridget had fallen
out of her bed in the night and
broken her arm and she also said
that Great-Aunt Bridget was
lonely and needed cheering up.

Mum gave us a big hug.

"I'm really sorry, girls," she

said. "But we need to go and visit Great-Aunt Bridget this evening instead of going Trick or Treating."

Meg chewed her lip and said "Oh" because she is a kind and understanding person, but I said, "We're not missing Halloween." And then, to show Mum I meant business, I said, "That is a fact."

(I am not kind OR

understanding, especially when Trick or Treating is involved.)

But Mum did not change her mind. She smiled, all pretend-cheerful.

"I'm really sorry, Mabel," she said. "But some things are more important than Trick or Treating and one of those things is cheering up Great-Aunt Bridget when she is all alone with a broken arm."

I glared at that mother of

mine.

I said, "Great-Aunt Bridget is not important to ME."

I said, "Great-Aunt Bridget is not even one of my top ten favourite people."

Mum sighed. "Mabel," she said. "That is not very kind."

"I know it is not kind," I said, "but it is the whole truth."

Then I stomped upstairs and accidentally knocked over a

chair (because accidents sometimes happen to me when Halloween is cancelled).

In my bedroom, I got into my werewolf costume and lay down on my bed.

I thought of Elsa Kavinsky's pumpkins.

I thought of Edward Silitoe's skeleton costume.

I thought of Sophie Simpson's

flying broomstick.

I thought, those children are so lucky to have such kind parents.

I thought, why is my mother so cruel?

A bit later, that mother of mine came into my room and told me it was time to get in the car to cheer up Great-Aunt Bridget.

In the car I looked out of the window. The streets were full of children in costumes. Some children had orange Trick or Treat pots just like mine.

When we got to the care home the corridors smelled of shepherd's pie and everyone spoke to us in baby voices.

That is why I don't like care homes.

Great-Aunt Bridget was sitting in a wheelchair in her room and her arm was in a sling.

"Oooh," said Great-Aunt Bridget, patting me on the shoulder. "What a wonderful werewolf."

"I am not wonderful," I said, all glaring. "I am cross."

Great-Aunt Bridget looked a bit confused so I explained my point of view.

"Werewolves are not happy if they have to miss Trick or Treating," I said. "Werewolves like Halloween even more than Christmas."

Great-Aunt Bridget's mouth

went ever so slightly twitchy.

"Ah," she said. "Yes, I suppose they do."

Meg gave Great-Aunt Bridget some chocolates and Mum asked if there was anything we could do to help her.

Great-Aunt Bridget didn't say anything for a little while because she was a bit too busy coughing but then she smiled at me and Meg.

I did not smile back.

I thought, Great-Aunt Bridget looks EXACTLY like a witch.

"What *I* would like to do," said Great-Aunt Bridget, "is celebrate Halloween!"

I looked at Great-Aunt
Bridget to check she wasn't
winking because when
grown-ups wink they are just
pretending.

I said, "You don't have a
costume. Elsa Kavinsky has a
broomstick that flies on its own."

Great-Aunt Bridget looked at
Mum and then she beckoned to
me and Meg.

"Real witches don't need costumes," she whispered in our ears. "Real witches wear whatever they like." And then she started laughing and I had to slightly grip on to Mum's hand because Great-Aunt Bridget's laugh was VERY, VERY witchy.

"The problem is," said Great-Aunt Bridget, pointing to a large china bowl on the top of her telly, "I can't hold my Trick or Treat bowl because of my broken arm. I need an experienced Trick or Treater to hold it for me."

I looked at the bowl.

I remembered that when it comes to Trick or Treating werewolves are VERY experienced.

Also, werewolves are quite strong.

I picked up the china bowl and I nodded at Great-Aunt Bridget.

"This is not heavy for me," I said. "I'll hold it for you."

Great-Aunt Bridget told me and Meg to hang on to the sides of her wheelchair. We helped

Mum push the wheelchair into the empty corridor. Then Great-Aunt Bridget told us to start running.

We ran so fast the corridor went blurry.

"Off we go!" said Great-Aunt Bridget, and suddenly ...

... we started to fly.

We flew past witches and wizards and vampires. We flew

through a forest full of ghosts.
We went all the way to the
moon.

When we had been going for
a long time, Great-Aunt Bridget
told us to slow down. This took
a while because Great-Aunt
Bridget's wheelchair was going
MUCH faster than Sophie
Simpson's flying broomstick.

We landed outside a blue door.

Great-Aunt Bridget knocked on the door and said, "Trick or Treat."

We waited but nothing happened.

"You have to shout," I told her.

"You have to be loud!"

"TRICK OR TREAT!" said Great-Aunt Bridget in a loud, shouty voice, and I roared (because werewolves can't help roaring when it is Halloween and there is a full moon in the sky).

Finally, a nurse called Bernie opened the door. Inside the room were lots of very old

people watching TV. Great-
Aunt Bridget explained about
it being Halloween and I roared
again to remind them and they
all started nodding and smiling
and looking in their handbags
and pockets. Me and Meg went
round with Great-Aunt Bridget's
china bowl and the old people
put in loads of UNUSUAL
things, including white mints

that make your mouth explode.
When our bowl was nearly
full we said goodbye and flew
all the way back to Great-Aunt
Bridget's room.

Great-Aunt Bridget told me
and Meg to eat as much as we
wanted. So we did. We sat on her
bed and stuffed ourselves full of
sweets and chocolates. Then, just

before we went home,
Great-Aunt Bridget
made her bed go up
and down on its own

BY MAGIC while we were

sitting on it.

It was

AMAZING.

At school the next day, everybody was boasting about Trick or Treating.

"Mabel," said Edward Silitoe. "Did you go to a Halloween party? I went to three."

I looked at Edward Silitoe for a long time and I took a deep breath.

"I don't bother with Halloween parties," I explained.

"I like to spend Halloween with real witches." And I told Edward Silitoe about flying in Great-Aunt Bridget's wheelchair and going for rides on her magic bed. Edward Silitoe laughed.

"Real witches don't exist!"
he said.

I did not elbow Edward
Silitoe in the tummy. I did not
accidentally tread on his toe.
I did not shout and stomp.
I smiled.

"Real witches DO exist,
Edward Silitoe," I whispered.
"And if you don't believe me I
will tell Great-Aunt Bridget

where you live so she can come and tell you herself."

Edward Silitoe stopped laughing straightaway and asked me to tell him more about flying wheelchairs. So I did.

Later on, Elsa Kavinsky and Sophie Simpson came up to me.

"Mabel," said Elsa Kavinsky. "Is it true you have a real witch in your family?"

Yes," I said. "Great-Aunt Bridget is very important to me. She is one of my top ten favourite people."

"Wow," said Sophie Simpson. "You are so lucky."

"I know," I said. "I am very lucky. I'm going to ask Mum if we can visit her again soon."

2

Magnificent Mabel
and the
Worry Box

In our school playground there is
a Worry Box.

If you are worried about
something you can write a letter
and pop it in the posting bit of
the Worry Box.

If you change your mind, you
can't get the letter out, because
the Worry Box is locked.

The key to the Worry
Box hangs on a hook in our

headteacher Mrs Roscoe's office.

Mrs Roscoe is a very strict woman.

Mrs Roscoe takes the Worry Box seriously.

Last week I put a note in the Worry Box because I spotted aliens in the playground.

I was a bit worried those
aliens might attack our school.
I was VERY worried those
aliens were homesick.

That is why I put a note in the
Worry Box.

The next day at break time
Mrs Roscoe came to find me. She
asked me to show her where the
aliens were hiding.

I took Mrs Roscoe over to the

big pile of leaves in
the corner of the
playground.

Mrs Roscoe
stared at the
aliens and her
eyes went all crinkly.
She said, "These aliens are
definitely homesick. We'd better
make a spaceship for them so
they can go home."

Luckily Mrs Roscoe is not always strict. Sometimes she is kind and pleasant.

I thought, it is a good thing that Mrs Roscoe is a noticing sort of person.

Me and Mrs Roscoe went to the scrap cupboard. We made an alien spaceship out of old boxes. Then we put the aliens in the space rocket.

Mrs Roscoe said, "If I know aliens, they'll be gone before lunch." And Mrs Roscoe was right. When I went into the playground at lunchtime the aliens had gone.

I told everybody in my class about the alien space rocket and after that everybody wanted to make one.

I took them to the scrap paper

cupboard in our classroom.

During break I made them sit on the carpet and showed them how to make a space rocket. Everyone sat still and listened to me. I was very interesting. I was quite firm.

But then SOME PEOPLE stopped listening and those people were Jordi Bhogal and Harry Cox.

Jordi Bhogal said making space rockets was boring. Harry Cox said he wanted to make swords instead.

Jordi Bhogal and Harry Cox started having a sword fight and then everybody else wanted to join in.

I was so cross. I kept thinking about all the poor aliens who needed space rockets.

I said, "Stop that" and then I said, "At once", because that is what teachers say when they are cross.

But Jordi Bhogal and Harry Cox IGNORED ME. Jordi Bhogal and Harry Cox

LAUGHED.

That's why I could
not help grabbing Jordi
Bhogal's sword and that is
also why Jordi Bhogal's sword
ACCIDENTALLY broke in half.

Jordi Bhogal was cross. "Mabel Chase," he said, "I am going to put you in the Worry Box for breaking school property."

I tried telling Jordi Bhogal that it was an accident but Jordi Bhogal is not a good listener. Jordi Bhogal went out to the playground and put a note about me in the Worry Box.

Then Jordi Bhogal started playing football.

I stared at the Worry Box, all wobbly.

I tried to put my hand

through the posting bit to steal
back Jordi Bhogal's letter but
my hand was too big.

I tried to open the lid but it
was locked.

Now *I* was worried.

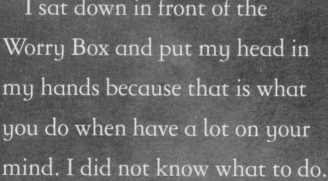

I sat down in front of the
Worry Box and put my head in
my hands because that is what
you do when have a lot on your
mind. I did not know what to do.

"Excuse me," said a sad voice.
"Is this the Worry Box?"

I looked up and saw a very small boy. His name was George Jones and he was in the year below me. George Jones's cheeks were red and his eyes were puffy.

"Yes," I said. "What are you worried about?"

George Jones handed me a note but I could not read it because I am not fluent at reading squiggles so I asked him to explain.

George Jones told me he didn't have anyone to play with.

George Jones said he didn't
know what to play.

George Jones said he wanted
to go home.

Then he started to cry.

I looked around the playground and I couldn't help noticing that everybody was already playing with a friend.

I thought, somebody needs to help this boy.

I sighed loudly like Mum does when she has too much work on her plate.

I thought, where is Mrs Roscoe when you need her?

I told George to come with me. George put the squiggly note in his pocket and wiped his runny nose on his sleeve. He followed me across the playground all the way to the sycamore tree. When we got there I asked him if he could keep a secret and George Jones nodded so I showed him where the fairies live. We played Fairy Tag and then we played Fairy Keepy-Uppy.

When we got bored of playing with the fairies I showed George the crocodile who lives by the swings.

I told George that the crocodile was called Mrs Moody because she is sometimes in quite a bad mood. I told George to hold on tight in case Mrs Moody tried to buck him off.

We rode Mrs Moody
through the swamp all
the way to the sports hall.

But then we had to
jump off Mrs Moody's
back because we spotted loads
of aliens hiding under a pile of
leaves. Those aliens told us they
were homesick so we went inside
and made a special space rocket
just for them.

When the bell rang, me and George popped those aliens carefully inside their space rocket and waved goodbye. Then George ran back to his classroom for afternoon lessons. He was smiling.

I slightly forgot about Jordi Bhogal's note after that, especially because when I got home I found out it was chocolate mousse for pudding and chocolate mousse is my favourite.

But the next day I couldn't help remembering again because Mrs Roscoe came into our classroom and asked to see me in her office.

I walked very slowly all
the way to Mrs Roscoe's office
because I was not in a rushing
mood.

When I got there Mrs Roscoe
told me to sit down. She looked
at me, all strict.

She explained that breaking
something that belongs to
someone else is not kind.

She said, "Do you understand, Mabel?"

I nodded and then I looked at the floor because I did not want to start crying in front of Mrs Roscoe.

I thought, I know she's going to make me stay in at lunch.

I thought, I wish she would get on with it.

But then something amazing happened. Mrs Roscoe smiled.

Mrs Roscoe said George Jones's mum had telephoned her this morning and told her that I had been VERY kind to George yesterday.

"Why don't you tell me all about it?" she said.

I let out a deep breath.

"Well," I said. "I was QUITE kind."

Then I told Mrs Roscoe the whole story in my own words because that is what headteachers like you to do. It took me a long time to tell the story because I didn't want to leave out anything important, but when I had finished, Mrs Roscoe smiled a bit more and said I had given her an idea.

She said, "I think we all need a break from the Worry Box for a while."

She said, "I think that instead of the Worry Box we need a Worry Monitor."

I did not say one word because

I was a bit too busy looking at the badge in Mrs Roscoe's hand. The badge was silver and it said "Worry Monitor" in red shiny writing.

Mrs Roscoe pinned the badge on to the collar of my T-shirt.

"Mabel Chase, you are the school's first Worry Monitor. I am relying on you to help anyone who is worried or upset. Do you think you can do the job properly?"

I stroked the silver badge and nodded.

"I thought so," said Mrs Roscoe,

and she shook my hand, just like
grown-ups do when they are in a
business meeting.

For the rest of the week I was
very busy.

I looked after everybody who was worried or upset.

Sometimes we rode on Mrs Moody and sometimes we played Fairy Tag but mainly I put them to work looking for homesick aliens.

Soon everyone in the whole school wanted to look for homesick aliens with me, even Jordi Bhogal and Harry Cox. We found loads.

But then SOME of those aliens
started attacking us.

We had to fight them.

It was a bit dangerous.

I thought, these aliens are
a menace.

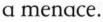

I thought, I need to do something before those aliens start taking over our school.

That's when I had a good idea.

It was a brainwave.

I asked Jordi Bhogal and Harry Cox to go inside and start making a big space rocket out of scrap cardboard.

I told them to do exactly what I said.

"You have to listen to me," I explained, "because I am Mabel Chase, Worry Monitor."

And I showed them the silver badge on my T-shirt just in case they had forgotten.

3

Magnificent Mabel
and the
Monster Scarer

There is a monster who hides under my bed.

That monster likes jumping out at me when I get into bed at night.

He hides in the dark shadows and he stops me going to sleep.

That monster is a menace.

If I had a brand-new high-up bunk bed I would not have a problem with monsters.

Brand-new high-up bunk beds don't have hiding spots for monsters underneath them.

Like for instance my sister Meg has a high-up bed, and she never has to run across the room and leap on to her mattress at top speed, because there are no monsters hiding under her bed.

The only thing under Meg's bed is a built-in desk.

Sometimes I sit at Meg's built-in desk when she is downstairs.

She has all her pens and pencils on that desk and she has a yellow chair with "Meg" painted on it in blue letters.

Next to the desk is a blue pinboard with Meg's favourite things pinned on to it, including a picture of Meg holding her pet rabbit Henry.

Meg does not even use that desk of hers.

Meg does her homework in the kitchen.

Meg takes her bunk bed for granted.

If *I* had a desk like Meg's I would use it all the time. I would work SO hard.

I would learn all my spellings in a jiffy and I would write out my times tables and stick them on the pinboard so I could look at them ALL THE TIME.

If I had a bunk bed, I would be a mountain climber. Or a trapeze artist. I could keep a close eye on my enemy, even when I was asleep.

Also, if I had a bunk bed I would not have a problem with monsters.

I ask Mum on a daily basis when she is going to buy me a high-up bunk bed of my own.

I say, "Can I have a bunk bed like Meg's with a built-in desk underneath?" And then I say, "Thank you very much" in a kind and polite voice because being kind and polite is handy.

But when it comes to bunk beds my mum is a teeny bit deaf.

I tell Dad that it is quite cruel for mothers to ignore their own children on a daily basis but Dad says, "Your old bed is FINE, Mabel." And then he laughs as if I am JOKING.

But my old bed is NOT fine.

My old bed is too low.

My old bed has a monster under it.

Last week I couldn't go to sleep because that monster was waiting for me to close my eyes.

I tried hiding under my duvet.

I politely asked the monster to leave me alone.

I started jumping up and down on my bed to scare him away.

But the monster stayed.

I thought, monsters aren't scared of anything, especially not me, Mabel Chase.

I thought, what I need is a monster scarer.

I thought, I wonder where you get one.

In the end I had to run downstairs and sit on Mum's lap in front of the TV until I fell asleep.

Luckily the next morning, the monster had gone (because the good thing about monsters is that they only come out at night).

I decided to do something to

stop that monster coming back.

I used my initiative (because that is what our teacher Mr Messenger is always telling us to do).

I went to the cupboard in the spare room and I got some feathery pillows and I pushed them all under my bed until there was no room for the monster.

That night I went to bed
all happy because I knew the
monster wouldn't be able to fit
under my bed.

But I hadn't realised that
monsters are really good at
fitting in tiny, tight spots.

Just as I was nodding off to
sleep, the monster came back.

I heard his tummy rumble
and that's when I realised he was

hungry and he wanted to eat
me.

I had to use my initiative
again.

I thought, if I feed the monster
lots of yummy snacks he won't
have any room in his tummy for
me.

I jumped out of bed and
ran down to the kitchen and
grabbed a packet of chocolate

chip biscuits from the snack cupboard.

Then I sprinted back upstairs at top speed and emptied the biscuits down the side of my bed, except I had to keep a few biscuits for myself because using your initiative makes you hungry.

Luckily, the monster was quiet after that (and even more luckily he didn't eat me) so the next night I put more biscuits down the side of the mattress and it worked again.

I did the same the next night and the next and the next.

For five nights I didn't hear the monster, not even once.

I thought, Mr Messenger is

right. Using my initiative works.

I was very pleased.

But on the sixth night, the biscuits stopped working.

The monster woke me up in the middle of the night when my room was pitch black. He made scrabbling sounds.

I shouted at the monster to leave me alone. I gave him more biscuits. I tried jumping around

on my bed just in case. But that
monster scrabbled ALL NIGHT.

In the morning I was very
tired and when I am very tired
I am sometimes ever-so-slightly
grumpy.

At breakfast I could not help shouting at Dad when he asked me if I had packed my PE bag. When Mum told me to go to my room to get dressed I accidentally kicked the table.

"Mabel," said Mum. "What on earth is the matter?"

I glared at Mum and I glared at Dad.

I said, "I am grumpy because

a monster kept me awake ALL night."

I said, "If I had a bunk bed with a desk underneath like Meg I would not be tired and I would not be grumpy either."

I said, "I am not keen on monsters," and at that point my lip went slightly wobbly. "That is the whole truth," I said a bit more quietly.

Luckily my parents can sometimes be kind and helpful.

Dad told me to show him where this monster likes to hide.

Mum promised she would tell the monster to go away.

I felt better straightaway because Mum and Dad are really good at finding things and when Mum uses her firm voice it is quite hard to say no.

I gripped tightly on to their hands and we all went upstairs to my room, even Meg. Mum crawled under my bed and started rummaging around and I climbed on to Dad's back.

"There are a lot of biscuit wrappers under this bed," said Mum.

"Yes," I said, and then I explained about feeding the monster to stop him eating me.

Everybody listened carefully. I started to feel a bit better.

"Tell that monster he isn't welcome," I said, all cheerful. "And don't forget to be firm."

But Mum was not firm. Mum
jumped out from under the
bed and shrieked. Mum had a
worried expression on her face.

"Mabel," she said. "It isn't a
monster keeping you awake at
night. It's a mouse. In fact ..."

Mum's shoulders went slightly shuddery.

"... it's lots of mice!"

At that moment a tiny mouse ran across my bedroom floor.

I crawled under my bed. At
first I couldn't see anything
because it was quite dark but
then I looked inside one of the
old pillows and inside were

thirteen tiny mice (I am one
hundred per cent sure about this
because I counted them using
all of my fingers and some of my
toes).

"Hello, mice," I said. "Thank you for scaring the monster away for me."

I told the mice not to worry about all the shrieking.

"My mum is scared of you," I said. "I don't know why."

I carefully picked up the pillow and carried it into the middle of my room.

I started thinking about all

the fun things I could do with
my thirteen pet mice, like for
instance I could train them to be
a showstopping circus act. I was
so happy.

But Mum ruined my happy
mood. She said we had to take
those mice out into the garden
and set them free. She said I had
to stop putting chocolate biscuits
down the side of my mattress

because she didn't like mice in bedrooms.

I tried explaining about my showstopping circus act but she wouldn't listen.

She would not take no for an answer.

She was firm.

That mother of mine forced me to carry the pillow out into the garden and set my lovely mice free.

It was very sad.

It was a TRAGEDY.

Then I had to go to school.

Luckily, when I came home from school everyone had stopped being firm. Meg let me choose the doughnut with the most sugar on it and Mum and Dad said they had some good news.

"Mabel," said Mum, all chirpy. "If we get you a brand-new bunk bed of your own, will you promise to stop feeding chocolate biscuits to monsters in the middle of the night?"

I looked at Mum and Dad.

I had a good long think.

"Hmmmm," I said. "I am not quite sure. Can I just check something?"

I popped the last bit of doughnut in my pocket and crept upstairs to my bedroom. I put the doughnut on a pillow

under my bed. Then I waited.
I was very quiet. I was VERY
patient. I may have slightly
closed my eyes.

When I opened my eyes, I
checked under the bed and I
could not believe it because the
doughnut had been nibbled.

I went back downstairs.

"I've checked," I said. "I don't need a new bed. My old bed is fine."

Mum and Dad looked at each other, all surprised.

"But, Mabel," said Dad. "I thought you hated your old bed. I thought you were scared of monsters hiding underneath it."

"I WAS scared of monsters," I said. "But I'm not any more."

"Oh!" said Mum, all interested. "Why's that?"

I had a good long think.

I didn't want Mum to start shrieking again.

I used my initiative.

"I can't tell you," I said, and I tapped my nose. "It is secret information."

That night I did not have to jump into bed to stop the monster leaping out at me. I did not have to keep my toes inside the duvet to stop the monster biting them. I was not one bit scared.

I knew that the monster wouldn't dare come near me ever again.

Because I had my very own monster scarer.

He was soft and brown and he
had woofly white whiskers.

He was MUCH better than a
bunk bed.